Bangers and Mash
have been bad.
"I won't buy yo
any sweets," says Dad.

Bangers and Mash
sit in a tree
sucking their thumbs.
They miss their sweets.

Bangers jumps up.
He has a plan.

"Let's make sticky toffee
just like Mum makes."

The chimps run back
to the house.
Mum is shopping with Gran.
Dad is in the garden.

The chimps are
alone in the kitchen.
Oh dear! What will they do?

6

They get two tins of syrup
and two packets
of sugar.

They put the syrup
and the sugar in a pan
with some butter.

8

Bangers dips his finger
in the pan.
Mash dips his in as well.
Yum! Yum!

9

Bangers stirs the toffee
with a big spoon.
Mash wants to stir it
as well.

Bangers won't let him.
They fight and
the pan gets knocked over.

Sticky toffee runs on the floor.
The chimps slip in the toffee
and sit down.

Mick runs in
to see the chimps.
He slips in the toffee
as well.

Dad comes in
to see what the fuss is.
He slips in the toffee
and sits in it.

Mum and Gran
come back from the shops.
They try to help Dad up,
but they slip as well.

They are all sitting
in the sticky toffee.
Don't they look **sweet!**

Their trousers are all sticky.
Mum helps them on
with their best ones.

"They are clean!" she says.
"Don't mess them up!
Don't go in the pond!"

The chimps run
into the garden.
"Trees are clean,"
says Bangers.

The chimps climb a tree
and sit in it.
This isn't much fun.

But it would be fun
to try to jump
to the next tree.

Bangers jumps. Oh dear!
He's ripped
the leg of his trousers.

22

What will Mum say?
They creep back
to the house.
Bangers has his hand
on the rip.

Mum is out.
But on the table
is Mum's sewing machine.

What luck!
He can sew up the trousers
before Mum gets back.

It's fun
on the sewing machine.
You can sew fast on it.

You can sew up and down.
You can zig zag across.

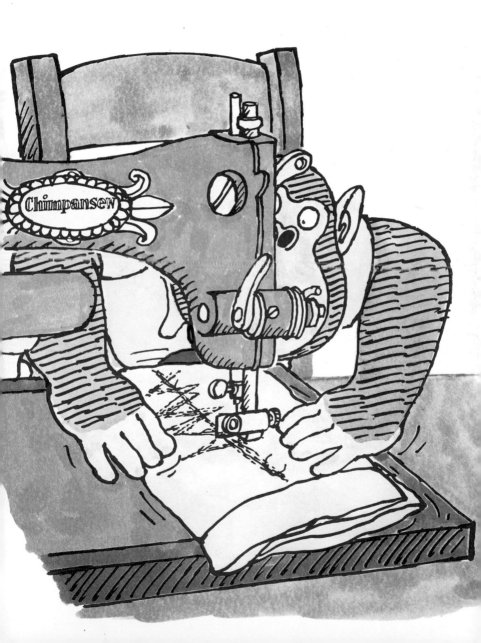

There!
He has sewn up the rip.
He tries to put
the trousers on.

Oh dear!
He has sewn up the legs.
He can't get
his feet down them.

And . . .
he has sewn his trousers
to his tee shirt as well!

30

Mash laughs and
jumps up and down.

Mum comes back to the house and sees Bangers. She laughs so much she can't be cross.